Copyright © 2023 by Puppy Dogs & Ice Cream, Inc.
All rights reserved. Published in the United States
by Puppy Dogs & Ice Cream, Inc.

ISBN: 978-1-957922-91-1
Edition: March 2023

PDIC and Puppy Dogs & Ice Cream are trademarks
of Puppy Dogs & Ice Cream, Inc.

For all inquiries, please contact us at:
info@puppysmiles.org

To see more of our books, visit us at:
www.PuppyDogsAndIceCream.com

To Oliver:
Every day your smiling eyes
melt my heart to pieces,
while your words inspire me
to think deeper and
be a better human.
I love you.

This book is given with love

To:
_____

From:
_____

Managing Our Anxiety
by Dr. Ying Wang, MD

Have you ever felt your heart pounding so hard that it might jump right out of your chest? Maybe when you had to do something new and scary?

That feeling is called anxiety. Anxiety can also give you cold sweaty palms and butterflies in the stomach. At times, anxiety is entirely normal and may even be a good thing, like before a soccer match, or when you are in a dangerous situation. Anxiety can supercharge your body so that you have more energy and focus. But too much anxiety can make your head spin with worries, and make it hard to eat, play, and sleep. Because anxiety can feel lousy, some of us choose to avoid anxiety provoking activities that may actually be fun and help us grow, or put off really important things. But anxiety does not disappear just because we ignore it, it always affects us somehow. In fact, the more we ignore anxious thoughts and feelings, the stronger they become.

The key is to not avoid anxiety, but find healthy ways to cope with it. Here are my suggestions:

First, we remind ourselves that anxiety is OK to have. It does not mean something is wrong. It does not make you weird or cowardly. Anxiety is a normal feeling that everyone has from time to time, a little bit of it can even be helpful. And remember, feelings do not last forever. Anxiety, too, will come and go.

Second, we put feelings into words. Find someone you trust and talk it through. Describe what you fear and be specific. Some prefer to write or draw – that is perfectly fine too. Turning feelings of anxiety into words (or pictures) can help make us feel lighter and freer. We may realize that our worries are way overblown, and things are not that bad after all. But even when things are bad, words help us put on our thinking caps, sort through what is really going on, and come up with solutions.

Sometimes, our feelings are too big and we don't have the words. In that situation, we move directly to the third step, feeling our bodies. Start by taking some deep breaths, drawing air slowly in through your nose and out through your mouth. Breathing deeply and slowly calms down your racing heart and makes you feel more relaxed. You can try focusing on your body one part at a time, relaxing each part as you go, until all of your body is relaxed. Physical activity can reduce anxiety by releasing feel-good chemicals called endorphins. Try going for a walk, playing a sport, or even some jumping jacks.

Sometimes, no amount of relaxation or movement is enough, and we really just need a good cry. In that case, let the tears roll.

Finally, know that there is always help. There are professionals who can help you get better at managing your anxiety – ask a trusted adult to help you find one. It can make a big difference.

Next time you feel anxious, come back to these pages to remind yourself: anxiety is OK to have. It may even be useful. You don't need to run away from your feelings – you have the tools to cope with in a healthy way!

Today, Andrew woke up uneasy,
His body felt shaky and tight.
He watched the sun hit the horizon,
And thought, "Something just doesn't feel right."

His stomach felt bubbly and queasy,
His chest felt all heavy and hot.
His spots felt too big and itchy,
His legs seemed to wobble a lot.

"What's causing this shaky new feeling?
I'm anxious, but I don't know why!
There is nothing that's wrong this morning,
The sun is still up in the sky..."

But still, Andrew felt so unsettled,
His friends all took note of his mood.
"You seem quite worried," said the rhino,
"When I feel off, I try eating food."

Chomping on leaves did not help him,
So, Andrew went along on his way.

"What's wrong?" Asked his buddy, the lion,
"I'm just awfully anxious today."

"When I'm feeling anxious, I try this:
I race through the grass and I ROAR."
"Yes, racing can help!" Chimed the Cheetah,
"Have you ever tried it before?"

"I personally like to go swimming,"
The crocodile said with a grin.

But swimming with crocs made him nervous,
So, Andrew chose not to jump in.

All his friends from across the Savannah,
Tried calming their quivering friend.
But nothing they offered was helpful,
He felt even more anxious, and then...

He could feel his anxiety spiral,
The panic grew deep in his bones.
He turned his long legs to the forest,
And ran off to be on his own.

Before long, he came to the water,
Where something was splashing about.
A hippo emerged from the river,
With reeds dripping down from her snout.

Her eyes were all reddened from crying,
And hot tears fell onto her chest.
"What's wrong?" Andrew asked the sad hippo,
"At diving, I'm just not the best…"

"The other kids make too much racket,
The splashing and waves are too much.
I can't see when I'm underwater,
And I'm scared of depths I can't touch."

Andrew then piped up, "Don't worry...
You're perfectly good as you are.
You may not be the best diver,
But I bet you can yell really far."

"I can." Hippo puffed her chest proudly,
"I'll add that nice thought to my list.
When I'm anxious, I think of some good things,
Around me in life that exist."

"It's nice to know others get nervous,"
The hippo wrapped up with a smile.
So, Andrew then grinned and felt better,
"I'm glad we could chat for a while."

"Today, I felt panic inside me," Andrew said,
"I was anxious, and everyone knew.
They all tried to make me feel calmer,
But the one thing that helped, was, well, you."

"You taught me emotions mean something,
There's a reason I feel them inside.
It's my mind giving me a new challenge,
It's my heart acting out as a guide."

"We can't always control our surroundings,"
Said Hippo, still trying to dive.

"But I'm confident I can do hard things,
Fear's a part of just being alive."

"Controlling my mindset is helpful,
When I panic, I try to stay calm.

I'll think of some good things around me,
And with positive thoughts, I'll swim on."

Andrew strolled back to the Savannah,
His legs were now steady and strong.
"I thought I could ignore this feeling,
But it turns out, that approach can be wrong."

"To be worried is perfectly normal,
Feeling anxious is something we share.
But if we kept our thoughts locked inside us,
We will constantly feel unprepared."

"Thinking calm thoughts is a great idea,
I'll keep a new list in my head.

And the next time I feel super anxious,
I'll try thinking those thoughts instead."

When I Get Too Anxious I Can Think About...

1. Watching the sunrise
2. How pretty the stars are
3. My favorite food
4. Singing a song
5. My friends and family

Although Andrew's day started poorly,
And he worried that his feeling was bad...
He could now tell his friends he was better,
Thanks to the talk that he had.

Andrew sure loved the Savannah,
It was full of adventure and sun.
And though some things made him worry,
Anxiety now wasn't one!

Claim your FREE Gift!

 Visit:

PDICBooks.com/Gift

Thank you for purchasing

What's Wrong Anxious Giraffe?

and welcome to the Puppy Dogs & Ice Cream family. We're certain you're going to love the little gift we've prepared for you at the website above.

CPSIA information can be obtained
at www.ICGtesting.com
Printed in the USA
JSHW071047020523
41129JS00005B/21